Mya's Mystical Garden

Tonya Warner

NEWMAN SPRINGS PUBLISHING
320 Broad Street
Red Bank, NJ 07701

First originally published by Newman Springs Publishing 2022

ISBN 978-1-63881-674-4 (Paperback)
ISBN 978-1-63881-675-1 (Digital)

Printed in the United States of America

To my beautiful and imaginative daughters
who helped bring this book to life.

Alstroemeria

My mom loved to garden. She planted all kinds of flowers. Personally, I found them incredibly boring. One hot summer day, not long after the school break began, I was watching my mom busily watering her flowers—again! Although it was summer, I wasn't feeling very cheerful. My best friend Victoria had stopped talking to me during the last week of school, and I was feeling pretty lonely.

Victoria and I had become friends after the time she had picked me first for dodgeball in second grade. I had never been very good at sports, and watching the other kids get picked for teams before me had been embarrassing.

On the very last day of the dodgeball unit, Victoria was one of the team captains, and it was her turn to choose. She shockingly chose me *first*, and everyone gasped loudly, which made it even more embarrassing. There were obvious whispers and snickers as I slowly walked to Victoria and stood beside her. It was such a weird feeling being picked first and then being able to peer back at my classmates as they waited to be called.

Victoria stood tall and wrapped her arm around my waist. "This is my best friend," she proudly asserted. "She is the kindest person I know, and I don't like how you have all treated her. And I don't care if you don't want to be on my team." We had been best friends ever since, even though some of the other kids were mean and called her Stinky Vicky.

I sighed. We had been best friends for all of second and third grades after that, but now, she didn't seem to want to spend time with me at all. I wasn't really sure what had happened, but now that Victoria wasn't talking to me, I only had my mom to hang out with all summer. And all she wanted to do was pull weeds and pour water on plants.

I rolled my eyes, and then I did something Mom always told me to never do—I picked a flower out of her garden!

She noticed right away. Gasping loudly, she shouted, "Mya, I told you to never pick my fl…"

But she trailed off. Why? I realized I couldn't see or hear her anymore. How had it gotten so windy? Where was I? I found myself surrounded by big old trees, but they were nothing like the familiar ones in my backyard. I could feel myself starting to cry.

Just as quickly as it had started, the winds calmed. A cool breeze swept away my tears. I felt a sense of peace, and suddenly, I wasn't scared anymore. I realized that I did recognize the trees, but they weren't the ones at home. They were the trees from the schoolyard. I looked down and noticed my hand was still clutching the flower I had picked from the garden. Because my mom had taught me the names of everything she planted, I remembered this one's name. "Al-stro-mar-e-uh," I whispered to myself, pronouncing alstroemeria.

My hand began to cramp from my tight grip, so I let go and watched the flower fall. It tapped the top of my sneaker and swiftly blew away.

"Hi, Mya!" a beautiful and familiar voice called from behind me. I spun around to see Victoria holding the alstroemeria.

That's weird, I thought to myself. *I just watched it blow away!* I looked up at my friend. "Victoria! It's good to see you!" I wanted to hug her, but she had such a sad look on her face that I hesitated.

She looked at the ground. "Really? You weren't so glad to see me last time we were together."

"What do you mean?"

Victoria pointed. I noticed that the schoolyard was suddenly full of kids. Students were sitting on blankets eating their lunches, so I knew it was the last week of school when everyone was allowed to have a picnic lunch with whomever they wanted. I waved at my friends, but no one seemed to notice me. Was I invisible?

Then I saw something really weird. Someone who looked just like me was standing in the doorway looking around the schoolyard. Suddenly, I realized I was reliving the last day of school! It was almost like I was watching a scene from a movie. What was Victoria trying to show me? I glanced back at her with a questioning look. She was still holding the alstroemeria and motioned for me to keep watching.

"Mya!" I turned to see Megan, the coolest, most beloved and popular girl in my grade, smiling and beckoning.

"Come sit with us!" All the cool girls with the cute clothes were there too, and I remembered feeling so excited that day. Usually, the other girls didn't like me, and since I hadn't been able to find Victoria, it had been really cool to sit with Megan and her friends. I had rushed to join them.

Then, I saw Victoria walking out of the school cafeteria with her lunch. She looked around, but when she saw Megan, she looked scared. I watched her slowly walk with timid steps across the lawn until she was standing right next to Megan's blanket.

"Hey," she said quietly.

I remembered looking up at her, at first happy to see her. But when I saw the confused look on her face, I quickly felt defensive.

"What? Am I not allowed to have other friends?" I heard myself say.

Megan burst out in laughter while the other girls joined in.

"Yeah, Stinky Vicky, we don't want you to stink up our blanket!" one of the other girls teased.

Victoria threw her lunch down and ran away crying. The scene faded away until all I saw was the empty schoolyard.

I gasped and turned to the Victoria with the alstroemeria. "Victoria, I…" I wasn't sure what to say. It made sense now why she had stopped talking to me, but I could feel my frustration bubbling up in me again. Why had she been so sensitive? Couldn't she have been happy for me?

She asked, "Do you know what this flower means, Mya?"

I shook my head and quietly responded, "No."

Victoria studied my face for a moment to see if the answer would suddenly come to me. When I said nothing, she told me, "This is the flower of friendship. Our friendship meant so much to me, and you really hurt me," she said.

Immediately feeling the need to defend myself again, I said, "*Meant?* Does this mean we aren't friends anymore? You are too sensitive, Victoria. Those girls were just kidding, and I really liked hanging out with them."

"I was hurt because you didn't stand up for me," she began. "That is not how best friends treat each other. We should always have each other's backs, and you didn't do that for me. Do you remember our gym class two years ago?"

I slowly nodded and looked down at my feet. Because she had stood up for me that day, gym class had been much more tolerable from then on. She had taught our classmates a lesson about kindness, but I realized that I had not treated her right in return.

A huge wave of guilt swept over me, and I began to cry. "I am so sorry for not defending you, Victoria. I feel like an awful friend." My tears grew into sobs as I asked her to forgive me. She stepped a bit closer to me, then retreated a bit. It seemed like she was torn between comforting me and teaching me a lesson. I felt so ashamed for not standing up to the girls who had been making fun of her. She was my best friend and would do anything for me. I understood that now.

I gazed at her through my tears and said, "I promise I will do my best to never hurt you again, Victoria. I feel so lucky to have you."

Victoria smiled. I really hoped she had for-given me. She didn't say a word but pointed over my shoulder. When I turned, I saw she was showing me a square. I realized it was my mother's garden. I turned back around to hug my best friend, but she disappeared as soon as we began to embrace. Confused, I franti-cally looked around for her, but everything was unfamiliar. It seemed like Victoria had wanted me to return home since she had just pointed that way.

I was confused. I wanted to see my mom and to be back in my house away from this strange place. But somehow, I had a feeling this was just the beginning of my journey.

I began to head toward the garden, trust-ing that Victoria had given me a sign. As I approached it, my hesitant steps turned into a jog, then into a sprint.

"Please, please, please let me go home," I whispered.

The garden seemed to have welcomed me, and for the first time, I appreciated its beauty. The same gentle breeze that I had felt before calmed me once again. I stepped into the garden, but I realized I wasn't home yet. This was a garden just like my mother's, but my house and my mom weren't here. I threw my hands in the air in frustration. I knew I had more to do.

Let's see, I thought to myself. *It seems as if these flowers have some kind of meaning. Victoria told me that alstroemeria means friendship, so maybe when I picked it, it took me to a friendship place. But now, I need a flower that means home.*

But which one should I pick? I looked down and noticed one of my mom's favorites. Begonias! Without hesitation, I picked the most beautiful one out of the garden.

"*Whoosh!*" The winds picked up again as I squeezed my eyes shut, hoping that I had chosen the correct flower.

Begonia

The winds stopped suddenly, and I cautiously opened one eye, then the other. My hopes were dashed as I realized I *still* wasn't home.

My surroundings seemed familiar but still not quite right. I saw several large buildings in a row with crowds of people walking up and down a busy sidewalk, but no one even looked at me. They all looked hurried, as if they had places to be. Still holding on to my begonia, I began to feel desperate for answers. Why was I here, and what did this flower mean?

Suddenly, a wave of people frantically ran toward the corner of the street. I curiously followed. I heard a bunch of people gasp and noticed a group of women, some holding their hands over their mouths. I tried to ask what was happening, but the woman I called to didn't seem to be able to see me. I guessed I was invisible again.

By the time I reached the corner, I realized what the women had gasped about. I didn't need to see it because I could smell it. There was a fire. And it was a big one. My dad was a lieutenant with the fire department, so the smoky smell was familiar and almost comfortable. I relaxed and pushed through the crowd to try to get a better look at the blaze. Giant yellow tape with the word "CAUTION" on it stopped people from going any further toward the burning building.

"Caution," I whispered to myself. "Caution. *That is what this flower means!* But caution from what?"

Since no one could see me, I stepped under the tape and approached the building. I recognized it up close. It was in my hometown. The burning building was the Main Street Factory, where a lot of our friends and family worked. It was engulfed in flames, but thankfully, it seemed that all the workers had made it out safely.

And then I saw him. My dad was leading the firefighters. I wanted to run to him, but I knew I couldn't. Instead, I stood there proudly, observing his leadership and bravery. His back was to me and was shouting to his fellow firefighters, "Is the back exit all clear?"

"Yes!" one of them responded.

"Are all of our men out of the building?" he shouted again. "The roof is about to collapse!"

"Yes!" Their response was a clear relief to him. But his relief quickly faded as he learned that our neighbor and his closest friend, John, had gone back in.

As my Dad heard the news that John was in potential danger, he pulled his shield over his eyes and turned in my direction. We locked eyes, and he put his hand to his heart, as he always did when he was leaving for work. It was our way of saying we love each other, kind of our own secret language. But how could he see me? I quickly responded by putting my hand to my heart too, still holding the begonia in the other.

Our sweet exchange ended as he turned to dash toward the burning building. Dropping the flower, I screamed, "DADDY NO!"

I waited in silence. Suddenly there was movement from the side door. John had gotten out! He was holding tight to a wedding ring. His wife had died not long ago, but I couldn't believe he would risk his life and my dad's life for that! I wanted to run to him and scream, "Where's my dad?" Before I could do anything, there was an awful noise as the building began to collapse. My dad was still inside! I squeezed my eyes shut and screamed.

And then…silence. The cool breeze swept away my tears once more, and I was back in the garden. Was my dad okay?

Caution. As I stood there realizing what the begonia meant, I felt that I had to go warn my dad. When I thought about it, I realized that none of this had actually happened. The real Main Street Factory was okay. My dad couldn't have gotten hurt, but I wanted to tell him not to go back in if it were to ever catch on fire. It almost made me feel kind of powerful.

Okay, here we go again, I said to myself, looking around the garden once more. "Pick the right one this time, Mya!" I bent over and plucked the brightest, most yellow daffodil I could find. As I had expected, the wind started right away.

Daffodil

"Happy Birthday to you. Happy birthday to you. Happy birthday, dear Mya. Happy birthday to you!" I heard my parents sing and felt immediate joy when I opened my eyes to see that I was home, although I had just missed supper. See? I knew my dad would be okay.

But something felt different. I knew today wasn't my birthday. I walked into the kitchen and saw my parents holding a beautiful birthday cake saying, "Blow out the candles and make a wish, Mya!" But they weren't looking at me. In fact, once again, no one could see or hear me. Their attention was focused on a tall teenage girl. I stepped even closer to get a good look at her face and was shocked.

Oh my gosh! That girl is me! I retreated backward as I felt my heart almost come out of my chest. I couldn't believe that I could see into the future, that I could see what I would look like five or six years from now. After I realized what was happening and was able to catch my breath, I looked more closely at the cake. It read, "Happy 16th Birthday!"

Wow, I thought to myself. *So this is what I am going to look like when I'm sixteen.* I actually really liked the way I looked.

I studied the daffodil still in my hand. What did *this* flower mean? I was starting to finally understand that each flower was teaching me some sort of lesson. Just like in my last adventure, I trusted that the answer would soon come to me.

The night wore on as I watched my birthday festivities continue with my parents. Mom and Dad seemed so happy, but I couldn't help but notice that the sixteen-year-old me seemed distracted, as if she just wanted to be alone. When everyone was getting ready for bed, I continued to observe my future self.

My bedroom in the future had amazing artwork plastered all over the walls. I was so astonished at the beautiful paintings of mountains, flowers and people. There were also dozens of empty paint bottles and used brushes piled up on the desk. If there were art supplies on the desk, that meant I was the artist! I suddenly couldn't wait for the future. I had loved to paint since I was very young, and I couldn't believe that I could see my dream actually coming true.

As I moved closer to the desk to inspect all of the paint bottles, I noticed a letter that was half hidden under a pencil drawing. It looked kind of official, so I stared at it curiously. The letterhead said, "Huntsville Art Institute," followed by a lot of content. I didn't read it all, but I did read the last part. It said, "For the final portion of the admissions process, please submit your best piece of artwork to show-case your style. Once received, our team will decide if you have what it takes to be a part of our college preparatory program."

What wonderful news! It seemed that the sixteen-year-old Mya should have been more excited instead of so distracted at dinner. This confused me as I continued to observe. Just as I peered down at my daffodil again, almost begging for an answer, my thoughts were interrupted by a soft ring coming from a cell phone.

"Hey, Victoria," older Mya answered. It was such a relief to know Victoria would still be my friend. But why was older Mya speak-ing in a whisper to her? What was she trying to hide? As I stepped a bit closer to the bed to get a better listen I heard, "I'm just going to do it. I *have* to. It's the only way I'll get in. My work just isn't good enough."

It was clear that Victoria didn't agree with this news because my older self grew more and more upset. It also seemed that she was trying to reason with me or talk me out of something, something very important.

The conversation abruptly ended. I watched, feeling worried. The sixteen-year-old Mya stood up from the bed, set the phone down on the pillow, and walked over to the art table. A pile of canvasses stood just beside the table, and she sifted through them. The shuffling stopped as soon as future Mya settled on a gorgeous painting. I held my breath. Looking closer, I saw that it was a painting of daffodils. Dozens and dozens of them in a field. It was one of the most beautiful paintings I had ever seen.

Wow, I thought to myself, *I can't wait to create this when I'm older!*

I glanced around the room again at the rest of the artwork and noticed that the same signature was on the bottom right of each one: MYA W. But the daffodil painting didn't have that same signature. In fact, a very small and barely noticeable signature read, "Honesty." My confusion grew as I watched.

It seemed as if older Mya grew increasingly nervous, and crazily enough, I did too. Our breathing got louder; our hands started to shake. What was happening? Just then, I watched my future self pick up a thin paintbrush, dip it in black paint, and paint over "Honesty."

"Oh no," I whispered to myself, suddenly realizing why we were so nervous. I watched in disbelief as she painted "MYA W." in the bottom right-hand corner.

Honesty! That is why I had picked this daffodil out of the garden, and that is what it meant. I so desperately wanted to scream, pleading with my future self not to cheat to get into that art school. It was the wrong thing to do. I thought that any of these fantastic pieces on the wall were plenty good enough to send in, and I was so proud knowing that *I* was going to be the one to create them.

After my sixteen-year-old self finished the disguised signature, she glanced at one of the canvases on the wall and took it down, admiring it. I could tell it was a favorite. So there I stood, watching the struggle between right and wrong.

"Do the right thing, Mya," I whispered. Just then, the strangest thing happened. She jerked her head up as if she could hear me. Startled, I dropped the daffodil on the bedroom floor.

The familiar winds started to pick up again, and I immediately knew where I was headed—back to the garden. I turned back to get one more look at my future self and could not believe my eyes. She was holding my daffodil.

Gladiolus

Once again, I searched the garden, but this time, I found myself beginning to grow weary. As much as I had started to enjoy my crazy adventures, my heart longed to be home. My tired eyes settled on the tallest flower I could find, a gladiolus.

I wasn't sure how long my eyes were closed as the winds continued to blow past me. When I opened my eyes, I found that I was lying in an empty field filled with tall green grasses that were dancing in the breeze. The sun soaked my body in warmth as I mustered the energy to sit up and look around, still clutching to the gladiolus. Waiting to see what this next adventure would show me, I rose to my feet and looked around.

Unsure of which direction to go, I began to walk and couldn't help but notice how hot it was. Beads of sweat began to form on my brow as I made my way through the grass. I walked for several minutes before I noticed the tall grasses becoming shorter. A small figure was standing at the end of the lawn, waiting for me.

She appeared to be six or seven years old and had skin a lot darker than mine. Cheerfully, she said, "Hi! My name is Ruby. You picked a beautiful gladiolus!" She began to twirl in her white dress like a little ballerina.

"Thank you," I murmured. "I'm Mya. Where am I?"

"Oh, I know who you are," she said, continuing her twirling. "I've been waiting for you. We are in the south, far away from your home. It's hot here, isn't it?"

I quickly responded, "Yes, but how do you know m—"

My question was interrupted as she continued, "I told you, I've been waiting for you, Mya. You picked that flower, and I am here to show you what it means. Come with me."

We began to walk on the hot pavement, heading toward what appeared to be a small town. The heat didn't seem to bother Ruby a bit as she continued to happily skip along, talking nonstop about her friends and family. She was so sweet!

Ruby took a quick turn and led me into a small jewelry store. The owner wore a sleek gray suit, which matched his thick gray hair and mustache. Again, I was invisible, and it appeared that Ruby was invisible too. The store was scattered with men and women busily surveying the shiny treasures. There was excitement in the air, especially for a man and woman who were looking at diamond rings.

"Ooh, look at these, honey!" I heard the woman say. "Can you take those out so I can try them on?"

"Of course," the employee said as he unlocked the glass cabinet to grab the rings she had chosen.

A warm breeze rushed into the store when a tall African American man came through the glass doors. Everyone, including the store owner, had their eyes glued to him as he made his way toward the diamond rings, close to where the couple sat.

"Ruby," I asked, "why is everyone staring at him?"

"Keep watching," she replied.

The store employee who was helping the couple looked up from the rings and informed the man that he would be with him momentarily.

Politely nodding, the African American man continued to look at the rings through the glass, smiling at the excited man and woman next to him. They didn't smile back.

Suddenly, a stout older woman was overcome by the heat and fainted in front of the store owner. The black man turned to the lady as people began gasping and rushing around.

"Keep watching over here," Ruby instructed, pointing back to the couple and employee. "Your question about the gladiolus will soon be answered."

The store patrons were asked to leave so that the poor and embarrassed lady could be tended to. Soon after, the couple began to stand up to leave as well, thanking the employee. The black man next to them also turned to exit at the same time.

Just then, Ruby and I witnessed something that no one else saw. The employee who had helped the couple slipped one of the diamond rings into his coat pocket as he put the other one away. Suddenly, he shouted, "One of the diamonds is missing! That black man took it!"

I could not believe what we had just seen! *He* was the one who had stolen it! The store owner rushed out of the store and grabbed the black man, who had only taken a few steps down the street. We watched out the window as the two men argued. Almost immediately, two police officers came around the corner and handcuffed the black man before putting him in their squad car.

Turning to Ruby with tears in my eyes, I exclaimed, "But he didn't do it!" Even worse, several of the store customers who remained on the street told the officers they had seen him steal it! "How could they accuse him when they didn't even see him do it, Ruby?"

She calmly turned to face me and explained, "It was because of the color of his skin, Mya. That man was my father, and all he was trying to do was buy an anniversary ring for my mother. He was arrested for no reason."

"I'm still confused," I confessed. "How am I supposed to understand what this gladiolus means? This is all so unfair."

Ruby studied my face. Victoria had given me the same look, like she was waiting to see if I would figure out the answer myself. Once again, I did not. Ruby continued, "I'm going to ask you something, and I really want you to think long and hard at what your answer would be," she began. "If you were *actually* in the store and saw the employee take the ring, what would you do? *Everyone* was convinced it was my father who stole it. No one even questioned whether or not it could've been someone else. Would you tell someone? Do you think they would even believe you if you did? Think about it."

I looked down at my feet, immediately feeling uncomfortable. I was almost too embarrassed to admit it. "I'm sorry, Ruby, but I think I would have been too afraid to say anything."

"I know, Mya. I know." She slowly reached her hand over to mine, gently taking the gladiolus out of my hand. "This beautiful flower means 'strength of character.' Do you understand what that means?"

Softly, I replied, still feeling ashamed, "I'm really not sure."

"Strength of character means standing up for what is right, no matter who disagrees with you. It means that you show integrity, compassion, and empathy for those around you. It may not always be the most *popular* choice, but having that strength of character will always be the *right* choice. Isn't that how you want to live your life?"

I nodded in agreement, amazed at how smart and understanding she was even though she was a few years younger than me.

She continued, "Did you know that long ago, black kids weren't allowed to attend the same schools as white kids? They weren't even allowed to ride the same bus or drink from the same drinking fountains. They were treated horribly and constantly disrespected."

"Yes," I replied. "I learned about that in my history class."

"Well, you see, Mya, not much has changed, has it?" she said. "We learn from our history books, but black people are *still* treated unfairly. And it happens every single day. I want you to remember this moment. Throughout the course of your lifetime, you are going to see racial injustice. I hope and pray that you will have the strength in your character to stand up for what is right. I also beg that you will lead by example and that the people around you will do the same."

Ruby gently placed the flower back in my hand, smiled, and walked away. I started to follow her out the door, then down the street. Once I rounded the corner, she was gone.

Letting out a long, sad sigh, I turned to head back toward the jewelry store. I had no idea where to go or what to do! All I knew was that I had to remember this moment. It was Ruby's desperate plea. As I passed the store one more time, I glanced up at the sign. It read Gladiolus Jewelry of Georgia.

I decided to try to find my way back to the grassy field but had no idea where it was. Desperately wishing for Ruby to help me, I began to run, dropping the flower. I wasn't really sure what possessed me to, but for some reason, it made me feel free. I wanted to let go of the sadness and shame I felt at seeing Ruby's father get arrested. I wanted to cry and scream and release some of my frustration, and running felt like the only way to do that. But most importantly, I wanted to go home.

My running came to a quick end as I accidentally stumbled upon the field. Looking around for Ruby one more time, I carefully stepped back into the grass and felt the rush of winds return me to the garden.

The fragrance of the flowers seemed so much stronger this time. Maybe I had never noticed it before, but it smelled amazing. I wished I could tell my mother how much I loved the garden's beauty and splendor now. I was beginning to understand why she loved it. Closing my eyes and praying my adventure was soon coming to an end, I bent down and carefully plucked a purple hyacinth.

Hyacinth

The wind sounded different this time. The last few times, the breeze had been warm and comforting in some way, but this time, it seemed as if the wind had a voice. It was a man's voice. At first, it was a low, echoing whisper; but then, it changed into a clear, familiar sound. I found myself turning in circles to figure out where the voice was coming from.

"Ah, there you are!" The man's voice was getting closer. I could barely make out the silhouette of a tall, older man approaching me from what appeared to be a worn farmhouse. As he got closer, I could see that he was wearing a mesh baseball cap, a red-and-black flannel shirt, baggy jeans, and work boots. He looked like he had just been working based on how dirty his jeans were.

"Aren't you a sight for sore eyes!" he exclaimed. "I suppose you don't remember me, do you, Mya?" he asked, slowly taking off his baseball hat to reveal his thinning hair.

He reminded me of someone, but I didn't know who. "I'm sorry, sir," I replied. "I don't."

"I didn't think so." His response sounded more like a sigh, "It's okay. I am quite certain she didn't talk too much about me. And we met you when you were a little one, so it makes sense that you don't remember." His shoulders slumped in obvious disappointment. "It was just wishful thinking that she might have spoken about me or showed you pictures."

I continued to study his face. How did this stranger know me?

Mustering the nerve to stand tall, he announced, "My name is James, but you used to call me Poppy. I'm your grandfather, Mya."

I stood there, not really knowing what to say or do. Was I supposed to smile, run to him, act excited to see him? My mother barely spoke of her father, and when she did, she would be very vague. I knew they didn't have a good relationship and that we hadn't gone to his funeral when he died, but that was it. In that moment, I could only manage a weak response. "Oh…hi, Poppy."

His sad expression changed a bit, and he smiled warmly. "Gosh, it's so good to hear you call me that again, Mya. I've missed you so much." He began to walk, gesturing for me to walk alongside him.

Feeling unsure what to do, I cautiously stepped forward, then hesitated. Poppy noticed and began to plead, "I understand you might be a little confused right now, Mya, and I respect that. But I really need to talk with you and explain why you're holding that purple flower."

I glanced down at the hyacinth still clutched in my grip and began to follow him toward the farmhouse. As we got closer, I couldn't help but notice the remnants of what used to be a garden. It hadn't been cared for in a long time and was full of dead flowers and overgrown weeds. It made me feel sad. It was so the opposite of my mother's garden.

We didn't say much on the walk to the farmhouse. There was an uncomfortable silence except for the occasional cough from Poppy.

When we walked up the steps into the farmhouse, I had a feeling I had been there before. The walls were covered with what seemed to be hundreds of framed photographs. Some were of a much younger version of Poppy standing alone in front of the farmhouse, and some were of him and a woman. There were many others that showed a young girl riding a horse, fishing in a lake, and planting flowers in a garden with the woman. They all seemed like happy memories.

Poppy patiently watched me while I studied the photos, waiting for me to ask him questions. I didn't know where to begin.

He began, pointing to a photo of him and the woman. "That was your grandmother, the love of my life. Her name was Emma. Sadly, she passed away very young, way before you were born, Mya."

Next, he motioned to the collection of photos of the young girl and continued, "And that little girl there is your mother. She's about your age in this one. Don't you think you look alike?"

I nodded, squinting so I could focus more closely on my mother's young face.

"Take a look at this one," he added, pointing to the photo of my mom and grandmother in the garden. "See what your mother is holding?" There she stood, smiling proudly at the camera, arm outstretched with a purple hyacinth in her little hand.

"So what does this all mean?" I asked, finally breaking my silence. "Why am I here?"

After a long pause, Poppy took a deep breath and said, "I know you've been on a long journey, Mya, and I am going to take you home. But first, I need to explain some things to you."

I was so relieved to hear that I would soon be going home. He gestured for me to sit down at the kitchen table, so I did. I knew I had to listen to his story.

"You see, Mya...I wasn't the greatest father to your mother," he began. "When she was a little girl, she was the apple of my eye. I even had this song I used to sing to her when she would follow me around the farm." He sat back in his chair, folding his arms and quietly sang, *"I love you a bushel and a peck. A bushel and a peck and a hug around the neck. A hug around the neck and a barrel and a heap. A barrel and a heap and I'm talking in my sleep about you."* He trailed off and cleared his throat, obviously trying not to cry. "Your grandmother, mother, and I had a great, simple life here on the farm. Your mother loved to ride the horses and plant flowers with your grandmother."

I thought to myself that maybe my mom loved to garden so much because it made her feel closer to *her* mom.

He continued, "I really thought your mother loved it here. I had hoped that when I got too old to care for the farm, she would take it over. But once she got older, she decided she wanted more. She wanted to go off to a big, fancy college, and I was afraid if I let her, I would never see her again. I just couldn't understand why she wouldn't want this life."

Poppy stood up to gaze at more pictures on the wall, settling on one of his wife standing alone. "When your grandmother died, all

I had left was your mother. And boy, did I try like crazy to hold on tight to her! I put way too much pressure on her to be exactly like me, and she resented me for it. She tried for years to put up with my sadness and anger over my wife's passing. I said and did a lot of stupid things that pushed her further and further away. And then one day, she finally had it."

He sat back down at the table and looked at me square in the face. He was sad, even regretful. Taking in a deep breath, he said, "There is a lot I am ashamed of, Mya. Your mother was as patient as she could be with me, but the last time I saw her, she shut the door for good. She brought you here for a visit when you were about three years old. She wanted you to see where she had grown up. But unfortunately, having her here brought back some very painful memories for me, and out of sadness, I lost my temper. I said things to her that were just plain cruel. So she scooped you up, got in the car, and I never heard from her again. I'll never forget how hurt she looked. It was one of the worst days of my life. I knew that I needed to give her some time, and I promised myself I would eventually try make things better. But…I never got that chance."

Realizing that he had never gotten the chance because he had passed away, I tried to comfort him. "I'm sure my mom still loved you, Poppy." I couldn't think of anything else to say. He just looked so upset, and it hurt to see him that way.

He put his face in his hands and began to weep. "I just wish I could tell her how sorry I am, but I know I can't." Looking back up at me with tears running down his cheeks, he asked, "Can you please help me, Mya?"

"How?" I responded.

Poppy reached for my hand and gently touched the tip of the flower. "This hyacinth means forgiveness. When you go back home, please tell your mother how much I love her. Please ask her to forgive me. I know it's a lot to ask…and I'm so sorry for that. But I *need* you to do this for me."

I really wasn't sure how I would be able to communicate Poppy's message to my mother. After all, I was just a kid. Even if she believed me, I wouldn't want to upset her, but I also wanted to help Poppy. I reluctantly agreed.

My grandfather's face softened upon hearing my response. He looked like he was at peace. "Thank you, dear Mya. Now…let's take you home."

Poppy held out his hand for me, and I happily jumped up and grabbed hold of it. I couldn't wait to go home. He led me back down the stairs of the farmhouse toward my grandmother's overgrown garden, walking slowly to take in our last few moments together. Once we got close to the garden, he stopped, turned to me, and said, "This is as far as I can go. Just walk into your grandmother's garden, put the hyacinth down, and you will be home."

I took a couple of steps, then realized I hadn't said goodbye. But when I turned around, he was gone. "Goodbye, Poppy," I whispered, knowing he wouldn't hear me.

I entered the garden and did exactly as Poppy had instructed, gently placing the flower on the ground. Almost immediately, purple hyacinths began to bloom out of the ground and surround me with magic and beauty. In the far distance, I was almost certain I could hear the echoing sound of Poppy's joyful laughter. He was happy once again.

Forgiveness

The winds picked up for the final time, and before I knew it, I was home!

"Mya, did you hear me? I told you to never pick my flowers!" It was so wonderful to hear my mother's voice again, but I was terribly confused. Why was I back in the garden? And why was I still clutching the alstroemeria?

"What?" I asked, looking at her sweat-streaked face. She put her watering can down and firmly placed her hands on her hips. Studying my face for a moment, she asked, "Are you all right? You look like you've just seen a ghost!"

"Mom...why don't you ever talk about Poppy?" My mom's hands immediately dropped from her hips. She didn't speak for what seemed like an eternity. I could tell she didn't know what to say. Finally, in a hushed tone, she said, "Because I was mad at him, Mya. Why are you asking me this now? C'mon, let's get in some shade. I think the heat is getting to you."

I followed my mom out of the garden, and we sat quietly at the picnic table under our large oak tree. I had so many things to say, but I didn't know where to start. I knew if I asked more questions about Poppy, it would upset her. But I promised him I would deliver his message. Nervously, I began, "Mom, I know you were angry with Poppy, but he loved you very much. He told me you were the apple of his eye, and living on the farm with you and Grandma made him so happy."

"Mya," Mom interrupted, "what are you talking about? You barely knew him. I didn't even think you remembered that you used to call him Poppy!"

"I know, Mom. But I know him now. He told me that you used to love being on the farm and gardening with Grandma, which is why I think you love to garden now. Am I right?"

Clearly confused, my mother began to shift uncomfortably on the bench. "Yes, Mya. All of those things are true. Gosh, I must have spoken about him at some point for you to remember all of that. Why don't we go inside and have a snack," she said, clearly wanting to end the conversation.

"No, I need to tell you something…it's important. Do you remember the picture of you and your mother in the garden? It was hanging in the farmhouse." She nodded slowly, staring at me in disbelief. I continued, "Do you remember the flower you were holding in that picture?"

"Mya, I think your active imagination is getting the best of you," she said, shaking off her stare. "I don't want to talk about this any longer."

"It was a purple hyacinth, Mom. A hyacinth means forgiveness, and Poppy really needs you to forgive him." My mother slowly began to rise out of her seat, then quickly sat back down again. I could tell she was beginning to cry, but I knew I had to keep going. I continued, "Poppy was angry the last time we visited him, but it was only because of how much he missed Grandma and the life you had together on the farm. He wanted to give you some time and space after you left, but he never got the chance to tell you how incredibly sorry he was. He's begging for your forgiveness, Mom. He doesn't want you to be mad at him anymore."

My mother's tears were flowing. I hated to see her so upset, but Poppy's message was too important for her not to hear.

"Mya, I am not sure who told you what happened, but it was a long time ago. I don't like thinking about it. It's too hard." She stood up again, and this time she didn't sit back down. "So…I've been craving some choc-olate-chip cookies. Let's go inside and bake them together."

I stayed in my seat. I could tell she still didn't believe me. "Poppy told me. I just visited him. I was at the farmhouse, and I saw Grandma's garden. Mom, it's all true!" I pleaded.

Mom slowly began to walk toward the house. She was done talking.

Quietly, I began to sing, "*I love you a bushel and a peck. A bushel and a peck and a hug around the neck. A hug around the neck and a barrel and a heap. A barrel and a heap and I'm talking in my sleep about you.*"

Just then, Mom stopped in her tracks and spun around to listen. "How did you know that song?" she cried, upset again.

"I *told* you, Mom. Poppy sang it for me. Please, I just need you to know that Poppy loved you so much and wants your forgiveness. Do you understand that now?" I begged.

Slowly, my mother nodded her head in agreement. This time, it looked like she was the one who had seen a ghost. Her face turned pale as she began to sob.

"I don't understand any of this, honey. But I do believe you. The only person who sang that song to me was Poppy." Her tears began to slow, and I saw her face begin to relax. Smiling through what was left of her tears, she continued, "He used to sing that song to me when I followed him around the farm. I remember happily skipping along, helping him with his chores. It was a wonderful memory, Mya. Thank you for reminding me. I adored my father and I miss him terribly…and yes, I do forgive him."

This time, it was me who stood up. I was so happy that she had forgiven Poppy. "Now, can we go make those chocolate-chip cookies?" I asked, smiling proudly.

Mom smiled back, the rosy color returning to her cheeks. "Of course. And thank you again, Mya. You're one special girl."

We walked hand in hand back inside the house and cheerfully sang, "*I love you, a bushel and a peck…*"

Friendship

Several days had passed, and we were slowly getting into the routine of our summer vacation. Mom would work from home and spend a few hours in the morning on the computer. Dad continued his tiring weekly shifts at the firehouse, and I found creative ways to occupy my time. As much as I loved the downtime, I was beginning to feel a little sad. I really missed Victoria. I realized I could do something about that!

Mom was hustling around the kitchen, preparing our lunches after her busy morning of computer work.

"Hi, Mom!" I said cheerfully.

"Oh jeez, Mya! You scared me!" she exclaimed, holding her hand over her heart. She giggled at the silliness of the moment. Mom was clearly in a good mood, which was typical when she knew she had completed her work for the day. "What's up, honey?" she asked.

"After lunch, can I go see Victoria? I really miss her, and we need to talk face-to-face. Can you bring me?"

"Well, sure, as long as she's home. Is everything okay? You haven't seen her in a few weeks," she replied.

I thought about how I wanted to respond to my Mom. I didn't really want to admit that I had treated Victoria so badly. "Yeah, well, hopefully everything will be okay once I talk to her."

"Okay, then I'll take you." I could tell Mom wanted to know what had happened, but she also knew that I wasn't ready to talk about it. I always appreciated that about her. She had a way of knowing when to give me some space to figure things out.

A half an hour later, we were in the car on the way to see Victoria. I was so nervous. When I had my adventure with her in the garden, I felt that she had forgiven me. But that also felt like a dream to me.

As soon as we pulled into the driveway, Victoria burst out of her front door and sprinted toward the car. Her smile told me all that I needed to know, and a sense of relief immediately washed over me.

"Hi!" she exclaimed when I opened my car door. I could barely say "hi" back before I was wrapped in her exuberant hug. "I'm so happy to see you! Mya, I had the *craziest* dream that you and I were in your mother's garden and you were holding a flower, and I explained to you that it meant friendship. And then I disappeared and then everything between us was okay! You're my best friend, Mya. I've missed you so much."

"I've missed you too, Victoria," I said. "I am so sorry for what happened at the picnic. I promise to never hurt you again." We hugged one more time. I didn't know it then, but from then on, our friendship would last a lifetime. We would be best friends through middle and high school. We would go to college together, and we would even be in each other's weddings. We would experience being parents and would always be there for each other through all of life's challenges. I was so lucky to have her as my best friend for the rest of my life.

Caution

It was another warm summer morning about a year later, and we were all sitting together at the breakfast table, excited to talk about our upcoming summer plans. Dad was quickly scarfing down his waffles because he was running late to get to the firehouse. He was just as excited for summer as we were. He needed a break.

"Wherever you two decide to go, I'm game!" he said in between bites. "I just can't wait to spend some quality time with my two favorite ladies."

Mom and I both smiled back at Dad. As much as he came across as a tough guy on the outside, we always knew he was a big softie, especially with us.

Dad realized he was running late, so he jumped up from the table. He glanced at me and gently pressed his hand to his heart, and I did the same. I loved our little secret language. Wiping the remnants of syrup off his lips and guzzling his last sip of coffee, he gave Mom a peck on the cheek and ran out the door. It was a typical exit on his busy days, especially when he was exhausted from the night before. As I got older, I appreciated how hard he worked for our family and our community. He was a hero.

Mom and I spent the next hour or so on the computer, researching all the different places where we wanted to travel that summer. In the past, we had mostly gone on road trips. We didn't have to plan much, and we enjoyed making new discoveries every day.

As we were settling on where our first destination would be, my mother's cell phone rang in the kitchen. It was my aunt, and from the sound of my mother's response, she seemed panicked.

"Wait, what's on fire?" my mom questioned. "Calm down, Michele, I can't understand a word you're saying!"

My aunt worked downtown on Main Street at an insurance agency, and she was frantically trying to tell my mom what was happening at the Main Street Factory. "Oh no! The Main Street Factory is on fire?" my mom repeated.

As soon as those words came out of her mouth, I jumped out of my chair. An immediate flood of memories came rushing back to me from my adventure in the garden. I knew I needed to warn my Dad.

"Mom!" I screamed, startling her. "I need your phone! I need to call Dad right now!"

Mom hung up on Aunt Michele, trying to calm me down. "Honey, he's not going to able to talk. He's probably on the way to the fire."

Immediately bursting into tears, I screamed again, "Call him right now! I need to warn him!"

She stood there stunned and confused. Not wanting to waste any more time, I grabbed her phone and called my dad.

To my relief, he answered, "On the way to a fire, honey. I can't talk."

Before he could hang up, I shouted at him, "Dad, listen to me. Whatever you do, don't go back into the building. John will safely get out after he gets the ring."

I spoke so quickly, I prayed that he heard every word, even above the sound of the deafening sirens.

"Okay, I have to go," the phone disconnected. Slowly, I returned the phone to my mother and retreated to my chair. I was so relieved that I had been able to reach him, but I still wasn't sure that he would listen to my warning. After all, it would have made no sense to him!

Mom studied my face for what seemed like an eternity. I knew she was just as confused as my dad, but she said, "Mya...this is one of those 'feelings' like the one you had last summer, isn't it? Like when you told me about Poppy?"

"Yes," I sobbed. "Dad can't go back into the burning factory to find John. If he does, he won't make it out. John goes back in to get his ring, but he makes it out alive!"

She rushed to my side, tissue in hand to console me. "Mya, I don't understand what makes you think Dad is in danger, but I trust what you're saying. He will be okay."

Minutes turned into hours, and we still hadn't heard from my dad. Exhausted from hours of crying, I rose from the couch and had started to walk to my bedroom when the phone rang. I dashed toward my mother as she frantically answered.

"Are you okay?" were her first words. Her face relaxed, and relief swept over my entire body. Dad was okay! "Of course, here she is. I love you so much." Mom handed me the phone and said, "He wants to talk to you."

"Hi, Daddy." My voice cracked as I began to cry once more.

"Hey, kiddo, I'm just fine," he reassured. "But I don't understand how you knew that John was going to go back into the factory. Everything happened just as you said, and your words saved me, Mya. I didn't go back in. John made it out safely, but the factory collapsed. Everyone made it out alive, thanks to you. I can't thank you enough, honey. You saved my life!"

His words made me cry even harder. It would be difficult to explain to him how I knew, but I was so thankful that I had learned what I needed to know to save him. I couldn't wait for him to come home!

Honesty

Six years later

It was my sixteenth birthday, and the last thing I felt like doing was celebrating. My mind was completely preoccupied, and the knots in my stomach were almost unbearable. Earlier that day, I had received a letter in the mail from the Huntsville Art Institute, one of the best college prep art programs in our state. I so desperately wanted to be accepted, but I didn't think any of my paintings were good enough to submit.

I could hear my parents busily scurrying around the kitchen. They had always tried to make my birthdays extra special, but this year,

I just wasn't excited. It took every ounce of energy to peel myself off my bed and enter the kitchen. I couldn't let them down, and I certainly couldn't let them know what I was considering.

"There's my birthday girl!" my dad exclaimed when I rounded the corner. "Where have you been hiding?"

"Sorry," I muttered. "I'm trying to decide which painting to submit, and I guess I lost track of time." Trying to shift my mood, I cheerfully said, "The decorations look great! And wow, that cake looks delicious!"

My parents smiled, but they knew I wasn't quite myself. As the evening wore on, I tried my best to not let my feelings show. But I couldn't wait to finish opening my gifts so I could retreat to the solitude of my bedroom.

As soon as the party was over and I could get away, my cell phone rang. It was Victoria calling to wish me a happy birthday. I was so relieved to talk to her. I needed her advice. She could barely get out "happy birthday" before I frantically interrupted her. "Victoria, I know a sure way to get into the institute! There is this amazing painting of daffodils I found at an art show. I can paint over the artist's name and sign mine! I just *know* I'll get in with this piece."

"Mya, are you crazy? That's cheating! If you do that, you'll regret it," she said. I could tell she was disappointed in me for even considering it.

"I'm just going to do it. I *have* to. It's the only way I'll get in. My work just isn't good enough," I explained.

Our conversation came to an abrupt end because Victoria had to get off the phone. I really wished we were able to talk longer, and I knew time was running out. I had to make a decision.

I stood there for several moments, wondering what to do. I thought to myself, *I'll just lightly paint over the artist's signature…just to see what it looks like. Yeah…that's it! Then I'll make my decision.* Bargaining with my own conscience, I picked my favorite paintbrush and painted over "Honesty."

Hands shaking, I added my signature. I could feel my heart pounding out of my chest. Could I really allow myself to do this? I put the painting down on my desk, slowly backing away from my potential deceit. The disguised signature looked surprisingly convincing.

Frantically looking around my room, I grabbed my favorite painting off the wall. I had painted it last year after my mother had given me a photo of my grandfather standing in front of the farmhouse. I had done my best to recreate the photo, and I loved it so much. It wasn't my best work, but I was so emotionally attached to it.

"Do the right thing, Mya," I heard in a faint whisper. Chills raced up and down my spine. I had no idea where the whisper had come from, but it was a clear message that cheating to get into the institute was not an option anymore. As I continued to search my room, I found a beautiful daffodil on the floor as if it had appeared out of nowhere. Honesty had won.

The following morning, my mother and I carefully packed the painting of my grandfather to send to the institute.

Two weeks later, my painting was returned, and I unfortunately wasn't accepted. But it was okay. I was okay. I was proud of myself for doing the right thing, and it only made me work harder. The following year, I decided to create my very own portrait of daffodils, and it was truly my most prized piece. Eventually, I was accepted into a great university, and after four years of hard work, I graduated with a fine arts degree.

Strength of Character

Ten years later

It was a humid summer day in Georgia, and I found myself desperately searching for something cold to drink as I walked through the streets of my neighborhood. I was twenty-six years old and loving my new life as a southerner, but the summer heat was getting to me! I had just finished my workday at the university and was looking forward to a nice walk back to my condo.

As I rounded the corner, I came upon my favorite bodega and quickly stepped inside. The cool gush from the air-conditioning felt amazing as I made my way to the drink cooler. After exchanging pleasantries with the cashier, I quickly grabbed my Coke and had barely made it back outside before chugging the whole bottle. With a wipe of my brow and a renewed spring in my step, I took a last swig and noticed something eerily familiar out of the corner of my eye. My gaze landed on a store sign that read Gladiolus Jewelry of Georgia. Why had I not noticed that store before? I had to have walked by it at least a dozen times! And why did I feel like I'd been there before?

My curiosity got the best of me as I found myself crossing the street to enter its doors. Mom's birthday was coming up soon, so it was a perfect excuse to shop.

For being such a small shop, the place was pretty crowded. Looking around, I noticed that all of the employees were busy helping customers, so I made my way over to the necklaces and waited for help.

"Ooh, look at these, honey!" I heard a woman say. "Can you take those out so I can try them on?"

I couldn't help but overhear a young couple excitedly trying on diamond engagement rings. Even though I had no idea who they were, I was happy for them.

A warm breeze of outside air rushed into the store as a tall African American man entered. Most of the people who lived near me were white, but people of all colors and ethnicities lived around the city. I was shocked to see many people rudely staring or frowning at the man as he walked up to the counter.

Suddenly, a woman fainted, and we were all quickly asked to leave the store while an employee checked to make sure she was okay. While the crowd of people oozed toward the door, I witnessed something shocking. As one of the employees was putting away the engagement rings, he slipped one into his pocket! At first, I thought that maybe he was just saving it for the young couple. What else could he be doing? I quickly learned that I was wrong.

"One of the diamonds is missing! That man took it!" he shouted, pointing at the black man who was quietly leaving with everyone else.

All the feelings of confusion, rage, sadness, and disgust rang through my body. Not knowing why, I managed to sputter, "Strength of character," and refused to leave the store. The woman who had fainted seemed okay, just a bit embarrassed. But I knew I had to stay to defend the man. I suddenly had what seemed to be a déjà vu vision of a little friend named Ruby, and I felt like she was cheering me on. A surge of memories overcame me. I had no idea what was happening, but I remembered my adventure with her. I could see her adorable smile and beautiful white dress. I remembered holding the gladiolus and the incredibly important lesson she had taught me.

"Miss, please leave the store. We need to attend to our customer, and law enforcement is on the way," said the store employee who had pocketed the ring. As we locked eyes, a look of fear came over his face. He knew that I had seen what he had done.

Resolute in my stance, I stayed put. Within what seemed to be seconds, two police officers came barging through the doors and asked where the suspect was. All the customers from the store had gathered on the sidewalk, waiting to be allowed back in. A little ways away, the store owner was firmly clutching the confused black man's arm.

Strength of character, strength of character... kept repeating over and over in my head like a broken record. I almost felt as if I were in a trance.

The employee began to tell the officers that they should arrest the black man, but I steeled my nerves.

"No, this man is lying to you!" I screamed as I pointed to the store employee. "It wasn't the black man. I saw this employee put the ring in his pocket. Check his pocket!"

As politely as possible, the two police officers asked me to step outside with the remaining customers. Again, I refused to leave. "Please, I saw it with my own eyes! You are accusing that man because of the color of his skin! He didn't steal the diamond!" Pointing to the store employee again, I yelled, "Check his pocket!"

They could clearly see the desperation on my face and turned their attention to the employee. One of the officers then stepped outside to check the black man's pockets, while the other officer approached the employee.

The employee retreated backward and yelled, "I didn't do it!" Then he tripped over something behind the counter. The cop reached down to help him up, but just then, the ring popped out of the man's pocket as he struggled.

"Oh, really? You didn't do it?" said the cop. "You're coming with me."

As the cop escorted the man out of the store, the other cop brought the black man back in. The owner trailed behind, huffing furiously.

"So this would explain the increase in missing jewels in our store over the last few weeks!" said the store owner to the cops. He turned to the employee. "I'm so disappointed in you."

Next, he turned to the black man, extending his hand in a hopeful handshake. "Sir, on behalf of my store, I can only hope that you will accept our sincerest apologies. It was wrong to accuse you because of the color of your skin. You will always be a welcomed customer in our store."

Lastly, he turned my way, thanking me for speaking up. I was so overwhelmed with relief.

The black man and I walked out of the store together, and I finally learned his name. He began, "My name is William. I don't know who you are, but I can't thank you enough for what you did for me. Not many people would have had the courage to do that. I wish I could give you something in exchange for your kindness."

Before I could say anything, he bent over and reached for a flower that had been growing in the ditch. It was the most beautiful gladiolus I had ever seen.

As he handed it to me, I studied his face. His light-brown eyes, smooth dark skin, and the tiny dimple on his right cheek were so familiar. With tears in his eyes, he said,

"When my daughter was very young, she had an obsession with flowers and their meanings. She taught me that the gladiolus means 'strength of character,' and that is exactly what you've shown today. Ruby was not on this earth for very long, but she would have been very proud of you, and so am I. I'll be forever grateful to you."

I couldn't speak. I watched him walk away, and I was almost positive I could feel two tiny arms hug me around the waist. "You're welcome, Ruby. It was an honor to meet you," I whispered.

As I was walking up the path to my home, a small patch of dirt caught my eye.

Hmm, I thought to myself. *This is a perfect spot for a garden!*

About the Author

Tonya Warner is a lifelong resident of New York, where she lives with her husband and two beautiful daughters. Her inspiration for the book was sparked during the COVID-19 shutdown when she began to reconnect with nature and all of its beauty. Growing a garden with her daughters while waiting for the world to reopen reminded her of how much there was to learn. Tonya and her family had been able to spend more time being outdoors and were curious about the meanings of many of the flowers and plants that she grew. When her girls expressed their curiosity and imagination about gardening topics, she knew she had to write something memorable for them.

CPSIA information can be obtained
at www.ICGtesting.com
Printed in the USA
LVHW022022190422
716634LV00006B/233